# VOLUME 1 - THE BEGINNING

*The Chronicles of Tikor*

Brandon Dixon

**Swordsfall Studios**

Copyright © 2020 Swordsfall Studios

All rights reserved

The characters and events portrayed in this book are fictitious. Any similarity to real persons, living or dead, is coincidental and not intended by the author.

No part of this book may be reproduced, or stored in a retrieval system, or transmitted in any form or by any means, electronic, mechanical, photocopying, recording, or otherwise, without express written permission of the publisher.

Illustrations by T'umo Mere.
Map by Brandon Dixon.
Cover Design by Taylor Ruddle.
Edited by Ianara Natividad

Library of Congress Control Number: 2018675309
Printed in the United States of America
www.swordsfall.com

*This one is for the fans. The world of Tikor is one that I want everyone to indulge in. I hope that this format makes the lore as easy to digest as it is succulent. Swordsfall is a setting and story for everyone, not just People of Color (PoC) looking for representation in their corner of media. The strongest and longest-lasting form of Change comes from the majority understanding the viewpoint of minorities. In a day to day setting, it's truly impossible for PoC to educate the masses. However, through media and literature, we can. So, I hope that as you dive into Tikor, you do so with an open mind and heart. And not just take the reading to mind, but to heart as well.*
*-Brandon*

# CONTENTS

Title Page

Copyright

Dedication

INTRODUCTION   1

CHAPTER ONE   3

CHAPTER TWO   9

CHAPTER THREE   13

CHAPTER FIVE   17

CHAPTER EIGHT   21

CHAPTER NINE   24

CHAPTER TEN   28

CHAPTER ELEVEN   31

Glossary of Major Terms   38

Books In This Series   39

Books By This Author   43

About The Author   47

# INTRODUCTION

## *What is Swordsfall*

*Before we delve into the land of Tikor, maybe we should talk about what Swordsfall is, for it's not just any setting.*

In a time where we know that representation matters, this project is an effort to add to the discourse in the way I know best. Narrative fiction in the nerdiest of flavors.

Swordsfall isn't just a story—it's a world. It's a dive into pre-colonial Africa for all the rich lore you've never heard of. It's an exploration into a world where most of the faces are dark yet aren't constrained to one corner. It's a world where women hold power equal to men and where the merit of one's soul is what propels one through life. It's a world where spirits aren't to be feared, they are to be embraced.

\* \* \*

In Tikor, deities and spirits are as real as the nature that surrounds them. Since mankind's earliest writings, the gods have been there with them. They make up a vital part of human societies across the globe. This is in a way to be expected. Humans were, in fact, created by the gods. Great deities formed cultures of their design and ethos. As time marched forward, these groups co-existed. Sometimes contentiously, sometimes harmoniously, but always striving to co-exist.

History, however, would change over the course of a tragic day and a horrific night. Mime, the Garuda deity of Wisdom, was assassinated at the hands of an alleged Vinyatian assassin. Mortals had never slain a deity. Tensions between the rival nations of Garuda and Vinyata soared under a long Tikor night, and a bloody battle erupted between the two sides. A truce was called once the truth was revealed, but not before both sides suffered irreversible damage.

Despite the armistice between bitter enemies, the wounds of that day will forever linger. The world heaves as the one constant, while the gods themselves waver. A new struggle begins.

* * *

Ten years after the bloody events that ended the Era, the world continues to recover, but the fallout begins to appear. Around the world, rumors spread of the arrival of a new kind of weapon: instruments capable of killing gods, Grim Arms. Could this be related to the unsolved assassination of Mime?

In Garuda, a power struggle swings into full effect as the current ruler of the Divine Order of the Phoenix, Amma Zencora, vies to hold onto his ill-gotten throne. How far will Zencora go to defend the throne he so desperately clings to?

Vinyata is adjusting to a world with one less of its cities, the Eastern Node having been destroyed during the war at the End of the Era. An unpleasant surprise emerges as they rebuild. The souls of those lost over the past 10 years have remained attached to the mortal plane for unfathomable reasons. Now, these malevolent spirits roam the region like an epidemic.

# CHAPTER ONE

*Tikor*

*A planet crafted on top of a fountain of unlimited energy, haunted by scars of the past. The world of Tikor.*

Tikor's most defining feature is its single, enormous land-mass. Its shape almost entirely breaks the world into a Northern and Southern Hemisphere. Life flourishes on these two massive halves. While the vast oceans host much life as well, most of the action happens on land.

The vast majority of creation myths take place on the land. While many cultures exist on Tikor, each with their own deities and customs, most of them acknowledge a single creation god, the great Divine Entity Ishvana.

She crafted the planet on a stream of intangible energy called Ether, one of the most basic yet barely understood elements of life. Every living thing has Ether within it and requires Ether to live. This flow of primordial energy causes diverse life to exist on Tikor.

\* \* \*

The great goddess Ishvana is as ageless as time itself, with powers that mortals will never understand. However, even she had limits to her abilities, as Life is not so easily created even amongst the greatest of deities. Ishvana crafted Tikor on a spot within the cosmos that supported her vision. To build a world full of life and wonder, she placed it directly in the path of the cosmic energy, Ether.

The combination of Ishvana's unknown powers and the massive stream of Ether, called Etherforce, allowed her to craft the marvel that is Tikor. She created not just the heavenly body, but also the life within it. The Ether flowing through the planet could empower generations of lifeforms.

Tikor's inhabitants would also be able to tap into the energy that had become a crucial element to the planet. For Ishvana the Gentle Creator, Tikor was meant to be the beginning. She had intended to craft more planets, and perhaps even extend the corner of the cosmos where Tikor resided. But before she could continue her mission, a rival deity interrupted her plan, Xavian the Withering King.

*Humans will never know what it feels like to be in utopia. To be in a state of perfection. And then to watch a monster show up suddenly and rip it all away. The planet may be here, but make no mistake, mortal. It's different from the world I was born into.*

— DIVINITY CADMUS DISCUSSING XAVIAN'S INFLUENCE ON
TIKOR

❋ ❋ ❋

Not all Divine Entities are like Ishvana, a being with the intention to craft and ability to create. There exist Divine Entities that truly enjoy corrupting and devouring what others have crafted with love.

Xavian is that sort of being, ever hungry to take from others.

Roaming through the known space, he corrupted as he saw fit, seemingly with little to impede his will. And like the harbinger of decay he is, the prosperity of Tikor caught his attention.

He gazed at what Ishvana carefully crafted and saw a playground of infinite potential. He wanted to destroy what she had created but not before corrupting it, bit by bit. The Withering King enjoys the slow act of destruction just as much as the savor of despair when he's done.

Xavian attacked from the edges of the cosmos, eating away at the fabric of its design and tasting his work as he consumed a path toward Tikor. Ishvana saw the impending decay and worked to protect her creation from the malicious force.

Legends say that though she had never faced a force as dark and twisted as Xavian, she remained steadfast in fighting for Tikor. She was every bit as determined to save her world as Xavian was to destroy it. In the same way that Xavian spread forth corruption, she pushed back with her own energy of creation.

Despite her best efforts at repelling his foul essence, he broke through her barrier that protected the inner galaxy. Her powers were great, but the Master of Rot had spent eons learning how to destroy. Now unimpeded, he launched toward the budding world.

❈ ❈ ❈

Once Xavian crossed her barrier, he immediately began corrupting the world. Ishvana fought back at every avenue, using her warmth to burn away his dark corruption. Despite her impressive defenses, the Withering King kidnapped a handful of the elementals Tikor had born.

He encased them within a second sun he created named Adume. In time, winged horrors exploded from the sun, the elementals having been corrupted into world-shattering Dragons. The horrific beasts set upon Tikor with their thunderous power. Xavian was strong enough as is, and with the Wretched Ones at his side,

BRANDON DIXON

the war started to turn in the dark god's favor. With her cherished world at stake, the Gentle Creator made the ultimate sacrifice.

Ishvana gave up her body on the physical plane to become one with the very stream of Etherforce coursing through Tikor. Using the power of existence itself at her disposal, she repelled all of Xavian's negative, corrupting energy from Tikor and the planet's plane of existence. Ryuu-jin, a former earth elemental turned dragon, returned to his senses when he touched down on the planet.

The corruption and Xavian himself were pushed into a pseudo-prison, Beneath It All. Ryuu-jin ordered for the imprisonment of the corrupted dragons, the Wretched Ones, and put his former brothers into an eternal slumber.

With the plane now safe from harm, Ishvana released her loving hold on the planet for the final time. Without her physical form, she became permanently one with the Etherforce. The ever-present guardian of Tikor.

\* \* \*

Tikor is a large planet with the perfect conditions for life. It has one central landmass almost split entirely in two. These two large halves that make up the habitable area have wildly different climates which very rarely fluctuate.

The Northern Hemisphere of Tikor is mostly temperate with warm to cool temperatures and heavy precipitation. This weather has led to extremely heavy forestation across the lands of Garuda and Grimnest.

The Southern Hemisphere, on the other hand, contains mostly arid desert with spots of sand dunes and oasis. This area of Tikor has been hit the hardest by the second sun hanging in distant space. Certain areas of Vinyata experience extreme heat, and strange weather patterns occur near the cursed lands of the Ebon Cascade.

The boundless ocean that nearly separates the two hemi-

VOLUME 1: TIKOR, THE BEGINNING

spheres is called the Grand Divide. It is home to countless smaller islands as well as the major island, the Independent Freeland of Teslan. The island nestled off the coast of Grimnest serves as a home to the order of Crystal Priests. The rest of the ocean remains a playland for Corsairs and other seafarers.

\* \* \*

Perhaps it's due to the strong flow of Etherforce flowing through Tikor. Perhaps it's because of the multitude of Divine Entities that came to this corner of the cosmos and created life. Regardless, Tikor is full of divine beings known as the Divine Class.

With very few exceptions, Divines exist on every land, in every country. Their presence has become a normal part of life on Tikor. While many of the world's inhabitants have excellent and friendly relationships with deities, not all humans are happy with their interference.

The nation of Grimnest, despite being to the west of the Divine-laden Garuda, has no gods or deities. Their absence is, in fact, a matter of pride to the Grimm, the denizens of the craggy land. No one knows why the land lacks Divines, though some suspect the living god mountain, Enkai, on Grimnest's border with Garuda as the reason.

Humans aren't the only ones that have deities either. The animal kingdom and its many creatures have their own gods. These supreme beings interact only with the animals in their domains and either have little taste in humans or outright disdain. These deities help keep the world in check, causing local humans to respect and even venerate the wildlife.

\* \* \*

From Tikor, two suns appear in the world's horizon. The planet revolves around the larger sun, Ila, and a second dwarf sun called Adume seems to shine only over the Southern Hemisphere. In truth, this second sun is a black hole. A quirky fate of reality, or a stroke of luck in the case of Tikor. For, you see, the black hole resulted from the cracking of Adume that birthed the Wretched Ones. When the winged horrors sprang from it to assault Tikor, the second sun's mass fell in upon itself and created a black hole, a horror of the galaxy. However, as fortune would have it, the black hole absorbed the released solar energy and the light around it. It reflected light back out in a similar fashion as to a normal sun, albeit with much less intensity. Why this sun seems to stay in a fixed orbit over southern Tikor remains a separate mystery.

# CHAPTER TWO

*Northern Hemisphere of Tikor*

*Sprawling forests and boundless mountains mark this a haven for the Divine.*

The lush, green lands of Garuda lie on the central part of Tikor's Northern Hemisphere. Home to some of the most forgiving lands in the north, the landmass took its name from the deity that helped curate the land and fill it with life, the Great Phoenix Garuyda. Also known as the First Daughter of Ishvana, she is hailed as the main reason why Garuda didn't fall to ruin under the might of the Wretched Ones.

However, the wounds Garuyda sustained while protecting her lands forced her into a slumber. The phoenix sleeps deep within a dormant volcano known as Mount Olenga—gathering her energy and nursing her injuries until the right time for her rebirth.

Many attribute the forgiving landscape as to why the Divine Order of the Phoenix flourished so quickly. The thousands of towns and villages on Garuda united over the landmass's bountiful terrain. Then, the Order established its authority and turned the nation into a cornerstone for prosperity. It should come as no surprise that the Divinity, Garuda's deities, had chosen the

BRANDON DIXON

founders of the Order.

The living mountain range, Enkai, serves as Garuda's natural border from Grimnest in the west. No one knows if Enkai is a mountain turned god or god turned mountain. The only certainty is that the range no longer allows passage over its spine. The mountains shake and howl at visitors, a reminder that those who walk up Enkai will never be seen again.

The Divines flourish in Garuda with the bulk of the north's gods living within its borders. No one knows the true number of deities in Garuda since the dense terrain of some remote areas makes accuracy difficult. Still, wherever you go in Garuda, you can bet on being near the Divine.

\* \* \*

The swampland and marsh of eastern Garuda give way to scenic cliffs and beautiful coastal shores. To the east of Garuda lies Hawklore, a land seized in the iron hand of its god-king, Hawken. While the nation may not encompass a large area, it's often breathtakingly beautiful.

Hawken decides the entirety of the country's tone and direction. He acts not only as the king but also as the nation's patron deity and founder. Little is known about the god before he created Hawklore, except that he once belonged to the Divinity. Eventually, the circumstances for his departure from the Divinity became the subject of many tales and stories. In the present, people only know that he has a plan to further grow his nation, and he'll do so by his own hand.

Hawklore also houses the only known inlet Azurean mine. This major fuel source usually only appears in the ocean where it grows underwater in large crystalline-like formations. The Blue Hollow, as locals refer to the mine, is different. The terrain has allowed seawater to flow inland and settle in a seemingly ancient crater. Anyone who falls out of favor with Hawken will find themselves toiling away at the mine for the "betterment" of Hawklore.

VOLUME 1: TIKOR, THE BEGINNING

\* \* \*

While Hawklore is an example of a successful dictatorship, Grimnest is an example of a successful anarchy. The lawless nation has some of the most dangerous landscapes in the Northern Hemisphere, from mountains cliffs with terrifying sheer drops to vast, unexplored subterranean caverns. It's a land whose beauty comes from picturesque scenery punctuated with deadly surprises.

Long ago, a King founded the nation of Grimnest. This founding ruler, in a dystopian attempt to control his people, inadvertently created the first pirate, the now legendary figure Lafitte. The King had ordered Lafitte's execution by sea, but he survived and returned years later with an armada of exiled Grimm.

Lafitte and his crew laid siege to the kingdom. They ignited a rebellion that led all the way to the capital. With his victory, the King and his family were publicly executed, their names lost to history. The crowd expected Lafitte to take the crown. Instead, as he ordered the crown melted, he uttered the words that became the motto of Grimnest.

"No God or King shall ever rule the 'Nest."

It should come as no surprise that, over the eons, Grimnest has turned into a hideout for criminals, pirates, and some of the most extreme cults. Yet, this chaos seems always balanced by figures who would stand up and fight for the people. The spirit of Lafitte lives on in pirates, raiders, and protectors alike.

\* \* \*

While the world has many hazardous places, most are still habitable by humans and most life. That is, except for the two places considered so hostile to human life called Danger Zones.

One of these Danger Zones, known as the Canopy, caps off the far western edge of the Northern Hemisphere. The land earned its name from its neighbor, Grimnest. If you entered through the rocky pass that separates Grimnest from the Canopy, you would be immediately greeted with the sight of impossibly tall mountains. They reach so high that the peaks pierce the cloud canopy above them. Something about the area has seemed to trap a perpetual ring of clouds that hangs over the area's numerous mountains. The sight would be beautiful if not for the danger. Perilous heights prove the most obvious threat. However, mysterious creatures rule the cloudy lands. While no one knows for certain, some fearsome predator stalks the mountains. Elder Grimm tell stories of dark shadows above the clouds—that their appearance over someone seals an unfortunate fate. People who traverse the Canopy, be it for glory or rare resources, risk never returning.

# CHAPTER THREE

*Southern Hemisphere of Tikor*

*Locked under the eye of Adume, the landscape of Tikor has been changed.*

A vast desert area dominates the Southern Hemisphere of Tikor, stretching nearly end to end. Nearly half of this expanse is known as Vinyata. The outer edges, the Outskirts of Vinyata, house the most inhospitable part of the deserts. Rippling winds, sandstorms, and nocturnal creatures plague the region. While humans inhabit some of the areas, the overall conditions of the Outskirts make it a persistent game of survival.

However, toward the arid land's center lies one of the greatest nations on Tikor: the Republic of Vinyata. The bulk of the Southern Hemisphere's populaces lives within Vinyata. The desert nation formed eons ago, around the same time as other great nations such as Hawklore and Garuda. The key difference, though, is that its progenitor is one of the most famous and divisive figures in Tikor's history, the defector dragon Ryuu-jin.

When Xavian dispatched the Wretched Ones to wreak havoc on Tikor, all the deities thought the Elementals were lost, forever corrupted by the Withering King's forced transformation.

BRANDON DIXON

But when Ryuu-jin, the former Earth Elemental, touched down on the planet's surface, his old self roused. During a pivotal moment, Ryuu-jin betrayed his brood siblings and helped Tikor's forces hold the line for Ishvana's final gambit.

Despite his reawakening, Ryuu-jin found himself alone and rejected by those he once called friends after the war. In solitude, the lone dragon settled into the heat-ravaged southern lands. He creating his own people among the sands, the Dracon. Through a persistence born of their maker, the Dracon have managed to thrive in a place thought forsaken by all others.

\* \* \*

Nestled in a pocket at the very southern coast of the Southern Hemisphere lies a kingdom in turmoil. The Principality of Ramnos has a new king, one which executed the former monarch, his own younger cousin. The citizens call him King Matan Longisus while Ramnos' nobles and dignitaries refer to him as the False King. The difference in the titles underscores the divide that has spread through this hidden kingdom.

Ramnos is wedged firmly, and securely, between the borders of Vinyata, the Ebon Cascade, and the ocean. A series of huge dune cliffs separate it from Vinyata, and an ominous gaping chasm cuts the kingdom off from the horrors of the Ebon Cascade. The poisonous mist from the Cascade's rancid waterfall leaves Ramnos' side of the ravine permanently marked—a grim reminder of the horrors not so far away.

This ever-present reminder guides and derails the nation. The former boy king, Rasan Longisus was only 16 when he met his end at his uncle's blade, but he was as corrupt as any of the Great Houses of Ramnos. The boy-king had begun to engage in a reign of tyranny that pleased the nobles and victimized the citizens. As a member of the Orchid Sentinels, Matan regarded his nation with the utmost pride. And as one who had seen the horrors of the Cascade, he knew how important its safety was.

14

VOLUME 1: TIKOR, THE BEGINNING

After Matan's coup, Ramnos now has a new king, loved by the people but despised by the nobles. Once a country who had sealed its borders to all outsiders, the new king has opened his nation's doors and allowed outsiders a new look into the small, beautiful and turbulent corner of the world.

\* \* \*

As far as humanity is concerned, the livable parts of the Southern Hemisphere end at the Twilight's Edge, the enormous chasm that keeps Ramnos safe, for on the other side of the chasm lies a land so foul that none dare enter. The Ebon Cascade. It, along with the Canopy, are the only two places universally considered dangerous.

In the Cascade, the evidence of its perilous terrain is immediately clear. From its eastern border, a series of foul waterfalls line its side of the Twilight's Edge. The poisonous runoff from the tainted rivers flows from the center of the area. The mist from the falls floats around like a curtain of death. The rest of the Cascade is elevated high above sea level, leaving a perilous climb for any foolish adventurers.

The area earned its name from its infamous skies. Adume's light makes the whole Southern Hemisphere brighter than the surrounding surface of the planet, everywhere except the Cascade. The sunlight seems to flow toward the area's center, giving an almost swirling visage of ever-present dusk that swallows light itself.

The Cascade provides the only known source in the world for an ultra-rare mineral called Shadow Obsidian. The mineral absorbs light when electrified rather than emitting it. This almost unnatural property makes its usage in Hekan arts extremely valuable. Moreover, Mali-Kar, the people of Ramnos, have developed ways to use it as a cooling device. This resource makes the Ebon Cascade an enticing target for adventures with more passion than knowledge, and most never return from their expeditions. The ones that do come back never come back the same. Seeing the horrors that lurk in the perpetual dusk of the Ebon Cascade isn't worth the mineral. No matter the rarity.

# CHAPTER FIVE

### *The Grand Divide*

*Savage waves and relenting winds make the Grand Divide a perilous journey for anyone who dares brave its seas.*

The Grand Divide is Tikor's single ocean. Despite being one body, the Divide is separated into corners, each with its own unique weather patterns. The large body of water to the east of the main landmass is known as the Santos Sea, while the body to the west is known as the Hunting Sea.

Many know the Santos Sea for its thick, early morning fog that paints the entire seascape in grey. It's most infamous for the choppy waters that it pours into Port Royale, the western bay of Grimnest.

The Hunting Sea, on the other hand, is renowned for its almost eerie stillness. Navigating on this part of the Divide requires careful planning as the open and still waters make vessels easy prey. The deep waters of the Hunting Sea contain creatures better left unstirred.

Throughout the Divide, currents can change at odd spots as the waters churn between the continent's two halves and then out into the open seas. They can then change again when the two seas meet deep in the ocean. These hazardous qualities make travel through the Divide a treacherous journey for any who go ill-prepared.

Despite the dangers, there are a number of habitable islands dotting its waters. The Independent Freeland of Teslan is the only one of a size and population count large enough to be charted. However, researchers estimate that anywhere from 50 to 100 smaller islands hosting human populations may exist. Even now, the waters of the Grand Divide have yet to stop humans from exploring its bounties.

❊ ❊ ❊

The only piece of land that keeps the two halves of Tikor from drifting apart is the Isle. The Isle sits at a strange nexus where it holds the world together and simultaneously keeps Garuda and Vinyata apart. That is, in fact, the origin of the nation itself. The settlers of this section of land declared it a sovereign state when its citizens looked to get away from the friction of the feuding nations.

Residents of the Isle have traditionally avoided picking a side in any large-scale engagement, something that falls in line with their founding dogma. The earliest settlers were merchants and craftsmen whose lifeblood depended on travel and inclusivity. The best decision for them, most of the time, was to simply not engage and remain neutral.

This approach has garnered the Isle a reputation as a middle ground for much of the world. If Grimnest is where the pirates and thieves go, the Isle is where politicians and merchants go. While many take this distinction as favorable toward the Isle, dealing with shadowy agents from the latter group carries much of the same risk. Many powerful figures reside on the Isle, and while neutrality may be a national policy, integrity is not one.

This strip of land-turned-nation is also a popular vacation spot. Not too many places in the world allow you to truly escape

VOLUME 1: TIKOR, THE BEGINNING

where you're from. The Isle is one of them. Its unique position has granted it some of the best weather in the world. Therefore, it's no wonder that the beaches of the Isle have become a hotspot for celebrities and other wealthy nobles.

\* \* \*

The other independent country in the Divide is the Independent Freeland of Teslan, a country devoted to the development of Crystal Priests. Located just on the other side of coastal waters from Grimnest, Teslan is an island-sized university and dormitory for its pupils. It's less of a country that trains Crystal Priests and more of a learning establishment with its own sovereign land. The chief reason for this arrangement stems from the rather unstable condition that allows Azurebending. The name users have given to the unique genetic ability. While the ability to interact with Azurean is a semi-rare mutation, individuals ultimately need training to use their abilities practically. In some cases, children with this ability need to be taught early on as it can seriously interfere with devices that depend on Azurean. This mix of gift and curse ultimately led to the foundation of Druse Academy, the governing body of Teslan. The goal was simple: establish a safe place for fledgling Crystal Priests to learn and grow their natural abilities. The significance of Azure makes the training of Priests not only vital, but often dangerous.

To ensure its safety against more adventurous pirates, Teslan has an omnipresent shield made from Azurean-powered Shield Generators and a line of Sentrylocks. A free haven to only Crystal Priests and those with the genes necessary to join, all others are ushered away from the island with extreme prejudice.

\* \* \*

Sailors say the Dark Spiral is the spot where the swirling waters of the Divide come together, creating an ever-present storm.

More spiritual folks say that it spews forth negative Etherforce, originating from a source connected to Beneath It All.

From afar, a dark spiral of clouds circles what can be described as a beam of light. Others claim they're just rays of sunshine peeking through the eye of a behemoth hurricane, locked in place by the crossing winds and waters. For every adventurer, there seems to be a new reason for the ominous storm.

Whatever it is, fierce electric storms and whirlpools of acidic liquid azurite keep most adventurers from getting too close. Those who have tried to find out what lies at the core of the Dark Spiral never returned to tell their tale. Even though there are no known survivors of any who dared explore its core, humans never seem to stop trying. The rumors of treasure and legendary items keep enticing more people to lose their lives in exploration.

# CHAPTER EIGHT

*Ila the Sun*

*Poised at the center of the universe, Ila gives Tikor life.*

While Ishvana and the other gods of Tikor get the bulk of the credit for creating life, there is one thing that stands above them all: Ila, the Sun of the solar system. This massive celestial body sits high in the sky at an unknown distance away. Its light and warmth truly make Tikor what it is.

However, Ila is often overlooked due to its more infamous sibling, the second sun Adume. Ila's gifts have been essential to life on Tikor, but the stories of Adume's birth and the horrors it brought to the world often overshadow perceptions of the suns.

After all, the effect that Ila has on Tikor is very real. The lengthy day/night cycle results directly from the long elliptical pattern that Tikor takes around Ila. Nevermore is the primary sun as loved or missed as during the deep periods of nighttime that accompany the winter.

\* \* \*

For all that Ila does, no one knows for certain how old it is. The creation stories don't often mention the primary sun, much less disclose the tale of its creation. A few Deities have been questioned about this over the eons, and the answers were never very solid. Is Ila older than Ishvana herself? And if so, what entity created it?

The oldest of the gods, like Ryuu-jin or Garuyda, cannot answer. The world hasn't seen the former Wretched One in eons, and the Great Phoenix Garuyda still sleeps within Mount Olena. The rest of the Deities, such as the Four Pillars and the Divinity, don't often speak on the matter either.

Of all the Deities on Tikor, no gods claim domain over the sun. This peculiarity adds to the theory that Ila predates Tikor's gods. Many of the Divines have or claim domain over various aspects of life. Be it bodies of water, ideas, or even the moon. Yet, none claim the sun as theirs.

While this quality went unnoticed for some time, recently there have been more talks about the curious nature of Ila. Is Ila, in fact, a deity itself? That would normally be the best answer as Tikor already has similar examples. After all, no one can claim domain over Enkai given that he's a god and not just a mountain.

The lack of godly domain has an unintended consequence. Strange and disturbing cults have adopted the primary sun as their patron. The thought that Ila is an ancient Divine Entity is a small sentiment that's gaining steam. For some, Ila represents the highest divine authority possible. In a time when gods no longer seem immortal, perhaps the sun is the only real god.

\* \* \*

Even though the age and origin of Ila are unknown, its effects on Tikor are not. Beyond the normal heating properties of a sun, small waves of intense Etherforce are sent streaming across the cosmos from Ila every few years or so.

Known as Solflashes, these small eruptions of cosmic waves

cause bizarre effects on the planet. Notably, Hekan spells may veer out of control. The increase in Ether in the very air can also cause some things to fail completely, smothered in a wave of energy. Conversely, it can send other devices careening out of control from a sudden increase in power.

The See'er spend several months every year tracking Ether activity in the air, adjusting their calendars for when the next Solflash happens. The Saltiguine announce these dates at the yearly Ceremony of Xoy where they give Solflash predictions for the year. It's not uncommon for merchants and others to tailor their year according to when a Solflash will occur.

However, there's a disturbing rumor afloat that Cults of Ila use these events to attempt to commune with the sun. No one knows if they are successful or not, but toying with primal Ether forces and deific summoning is never a good combination.

# CHAPTER NINE

### *Adume the Second Sun*

*The second sun shines brightly on Tikor, hiding its own secret.*

Nestled in the horizon, behind Tikor's first sun sits one of the few things the Withering King ever actually created, the second sun Adume. During the Withering King's battle with the mother creator Ishvana, he formed this second sun. In a ploy she never thought possible, Xavian abducted a number of the planet's elemental spirits and deities before encasing them in Adume. What hatched from this contemptible womb were no longer children of Tikor, but horrifying world-breaking dragons. However, with a twist of fate and perhaps luck, the dragon Ryuu-jin regained the sense of self he had from his previous life as an earth elemental upon touching Tikor's soil. He broke free of Xavian's mind control, helping to turn the course of the battle.

The fiery remains of the prison, still smoldering with raw power, became a second sun away from the planet. It serves as an unwanted reminder of Xavian's influence and a source of unremitting heat to Tikor's southern half.

VOLUME 1: TIKOR, THE BEGINNING

\* \* \*

The original sun sits at a fixed point as Tikor and the other heavenly bodies revolve around it. The cursed sun Adume, however, doesn't seem to hold a fixed point, nor do other heavenly bodies seem to orbit it. As far as astrologers can tell, Adume simply maintains a fixed orbit around Tikor that keeps its rays directly shining on Vinyata. Without Adume's influence, scientists estimate that the temperatures in the south would be 35 degrees cooler on average, possibly allowing the development of vegetation and other delicate life.

The second sun makes such a profound difference on the land that one could believe Vinyata was cursed if Ryuu-jin had not handpicked the spot. The Dracon say he did so to own a sense of his birth. The Karu say it was out of atonement. Though, many people may think otherwise if they knew what Adume really was.

Around a decade before the war at the End of the Era, Kent Musa and the Omicron Space Lab launched a surprise under the cover of night. Using adapted missile technology, Musa and his team sent a probe into space. For years prior, the pioneer had gazed up at the sky and wondered what could be. It took more time for them to attain a speed that allowed the probe to break the strange barrier around the atmosphere. With the adaptation of some Latimer drives, Musa successfully broke that barrier for a few seconds.

The data that they received forced the CEO to swear the entire team to secrecy. They pored over the data repeatedly to confirm its truth. What they had discovered floored Musa and his team. Adume was no sun. It didn't pulsate like Ila, the original sun. Adume was darker, different. The core body itself couldn't be detected, only the edges. They became the first to discover that the second sun was a black hole. A fact still secret to the rest of the world.

\* \* \*

Many have wondered where Divine Entities like Ishvana and Xavian come from. What created that which created us? A question too large for most to ask, let alone answer. One crazy tale has gone around for centuries, only believed by the most devout. It says that a man came across a puzzle box. Intrigued by the box's beauty and the detail of the puzzle, he set to open it. It would take him a total of 15 years to solve the puzzle, but when he did, he found one of the fabled Godheads inside the box. It awoke and offered to answer any questions. The man asked where the greatest deity of them all, Ishvana, came from.

The head gazed deep into the man and whispered, "From a hole so dark that only light remains, a place not for the mortal coil. Pray until thy death that the door stays closed." The image of the door appeared in the man's mind, rending him blind. Some believe this a cautionary tale about asking for too much. However, a fringe theory came from the quaint quip, "What if the gods came through a portal deep in space?" This theory usually devolved into the distance lizard people could travel, rendering it forgettable for most. What Musa found, however, put a light on the possibility.

* * *

Musa's team came up with a theory, or assumptions really, based on the brief burst of information they acquired and historical document. The womb that Xavian created most likely was not a sun initially. After Adume birthed the Wretched Ones, it collapsed upon itself. The force of the collapse may have created the black hole, or perhaps the black hole existed at the womb's center the whole time.

Either way, Adume had transformed into a black hole that began to emit light. It produced enough light to change the surface temperature of Tikor but remained far enough way to not destroy it. Adume has always been a silent mystery in the sky, a source of many myths and tales. Omicron had accidentally stumbled across answers and even more mysteries.

Omicron continues their attempts to break through the atmospheric barrier and gather more data, but all subsequent efforts have failed. While no one on the probe team doubts the validity of their work, no one is ready to go public without the ability to verify it. The news that the second sun may be something more is a lot to accept as well as brings up far more questions. Until they could collect further evidence, Musa ordered the entire experiment "Top Secret."

# CHAPTER TEN

*Omaat the Moon*

*Suspended above the skies sits the shiny beacon of every Tikor night.*

Nestled above Tikor sits its only moon, Omaat. Tales of the moon have been told since the beginning of history with every culture on Tikor having some tie the heavenly body. For some, the moon is the ultimate representation of the night and any life associated with it. For those on the sea, Omaat serves as an ever-present beacon and source of light. And for some, the moon is a symbol of worship, not just of the physical body itself but of any deities associated with it.

It's not uncommon to hear about "Omaat's Expression," a phrase that originates from the way the moon changes hues of color throughout its cycle. At its fullest, Omaat gives off a reddish hue for a day or two and then continues down the color spectrum, reaching a violet hue at its dimmest phase. Some people like the See'er are especially superstitious when it comes to the moon's phases and the effects they have. For example, some rituals are only performed during specific lunar phases.

While many around the world tell the story of how Tikor came to be, Omaat's origins aren't as defined. In fact, there isn't even a consensus as to when the satellite came into being. The Karu believe that the Supreme Creator Ishvana crafted Omaat after birthing Tikor. For them, she created everything involved in and around the planet.

The See'er, as masters of Cosmology and Astrology, heavily disagree. They don't believe that Ishvana created the moon. Instead, they claim that Omaat originated as a large asteroid captured by Tikor's gravity early on in its life. To them, it's proof that there are other beings in the universe capable of creation, especially given they credit their supreme god Ro'og for creating Tikor.

The Dracon, however, have another answer. They think that Omaat is a large chunk launched from Adume when it cracked and birthed the Wretched Ones. While many venerate the moon, the Dracon look to the sky with worry. For them, anything associated with the twisted elementals or Adume is tainted.

*   *   *

With the moon being an ancient celestial body, it's often associated with the loftiest gods. The most known of these deities is Naburoku, the Guiding Light. As one of the Mistoa, her domain over the moon is as much spiritual as it is physical. Her attachment to the Moon often manifests in a detached manner. Even Naburoku's worshippers will admit that sometimes it feels more like talking to a distant object than communing with their goddess. Most deities of Tikor tend to be very close to their followers. The Moon Goddess is not one of those.

Despite Omaat being a constant presence in the night sky, dedicated worship to moon deities has always been a fringe concept. The positive effects of the domain are often strange and meandering. It's no surprise that perceptions of worshippers range anywhere from absentminded to cult-like.

*   *   *

Omaat's brightness changes in a specific color pattern every month. These colorations can be seen so vibrantly mainly due to the extra light from Adume. The second sun illuminates the moon at even the most awkward of planetary alignments. So, no matter the phase or position, Omaat's outline always remains visible at the least.

This permanent visibility has made the study of the moon more scientific than spiritual, even with the existence of deities with domains over the moon. Tikor's denizens have a great fascination with its single moon, and humans unfailing learn more about its ever-changing tale as time goes by. The most interesting observation that can be seen with the naked eye is the faint ring of space debris that encircles Omaat. Recorded history shows that it did not always exist. So then, where did this ring come from? Researchers suggest that Adume's proximity has had some effect on Omaat, perhaps even trapping space debris between the celestial bodies.

Omaat takes on a striking appearance during all its phases. The most gorgeous interaction with Ila and Adume involves the various colors the moon cycles through. The mixture of Tikor's atmosphere and the two suns causes Omaat to shift through the color spectrum during its lunar cycle. The colors don't come through every night, though sometimes, the local weather can change the air enough to neutralize the color.

At its fullest, Omaat shimmers with a blood-red hue, sometimes giving the sky an ominous tone during the summer's fullest of moons. The color fades to dull orange as the moon shifts toward its half stage, where it shines with a transcendent greenish-blue. Then, it lights up into a vibrant blue at its final crescent stage. Once the moon can barely be seen, the colors end with a haunting violet.

# CHAPTER ELEVEN

*Beneath It All*

*WHAT NIGHTMARES DREAM OF*

There lies another world barely separated from Tikor. One in which the greatest evil known lies in wait, biding his time for the chance to finish what he started.

Beneath It All is the semi-universal name for the murk that lies underneath every evil decision, vile creature, and shadowy corner. That dark voice in the back of your mind whispering sweet malice to you is not always an illusion. Parents around the world have long used this primal fear as a cautionary bedtime story to scare their children, even though deep down they, too, dread it. The oft-whispered myth that Raksha, Xavian's horrific brood of monsters, seep through cracks from Beneath It All is as old as time itself.

❈ ❈ ❈

The mother creator of Tikor, Ishvana, sacrificed herself to protect her world from Xavian's corruption. Through her martyrdom, she severed the mortal realm of Tikor from the Withering King's corrupting reach. No matter the method, Xavian cannot directly affect the physical world.

However, this limitation doesn't preclude him from his goal of ultimate corruption. Where once he utilized his very essence to decimate reality around him, he now resorts to more indirect methods. While the Ether and the plane of existence that Tikor sits on is protected from harm, the place that Xavian now calls home lies just below the surface.

*Knock knock, said the shadow. The small child shrank in the dimly lit corner of his room. He hadn't meant to call the shadow. It was just a prank his friends at school had convinced him to try.*

*ANSWER ME, the apparition bellowed.*

*The boy wept in his dreadful ignorance. He hadn't wanted this.*

*It was supposed to be a JOKE. Through his fraught sobs, he wiped his tear-stained eyes. As his gaze adjusted to the darkness, he could no longer make out the shadow. He let out a sigh of relief.*

*KNOCK KNOCK, he heard as he felt the hot stench of its breath on his neck.*

— EXCERPT FROM "THE BOY WHO CALLED TO THE UN-
SPOKEN"

VOLUME 1: TIKOR, THE BEGINNING

Where Xavian dwells is a place that is, in essence, not a place. No mortal can visit it nor may any creature inside willingly depart. The dimension truly belongs to the Withering King, and he molds it and its inhabitants like moist clay. It's a place you can't go to, yet it's also right there underneath the soles of your feet.

It's not a physical realm where material existence is clear-cut—the rules are murkier than that. It's a plane that strange, ancient, and powerful forces keep sequestered. Some of the worse, nightmarish creatures ever created reside here, and a dark lord of corruption who rules them is just Beneath it All.

Ether energy only flows naturally to the Divine from the Etherforce itself. While mortals can harness this energy, they must call on it through their chosen deity. That call and alliance afford certain protections. Those protections involve a barrier that inhibits anything from other dimensions from interacting with the patron. But when that call and bond ceases, so does that protection.

Few humans realize that these bonds prevent Xavian's corrupting whisper from seeping in. He cannot physically interact with the mortal world of Tikor, but he can exploit any holes put there through alluring whispers of dark dreams and temptations. Intentionally, or otherwise.

\* \* \*

Tikor's lands are captivating yet cruel. This is no more apparent than the fact that when humans fall to their weakest moment mentally, they become most susceptible to corruption. It's not an overnight process, though. It's a slow, creeping degeneration that spreads, infecting the person like an unholy virus. When this corruption happens, the host starts going through a number of changes that include violent mood swings, extreme irritability, increased violent tendencies, and vivid hallucinations. These effects mark the onset of the hybrid virus and curse, Xavian's Touch.

\* \* \*

When Raksha are banished or killed, they are sent to Beneath It All. In a way, they return to their vile maker for judgment on their deeds and actions on Tikor—though more like a carnage evaluation with high marks for extreme savagery.

Some tales say Raksha may return when called by Xavian himself, but if so, no one knows how that is possible. Raksha can latch on and possess hosts corrupted by Xavian's Touch. While the Touch can be cured, a person can no longer return to being mortal once a Raksha has taken possession of them. Upon being possessed, ravenous deepspawn devour the human's soul, which leaves the human meat suit to the Raksha.

There are many horrors on Tikor, enough to almost balance out its magic and wonder. However, none compare to the Raksha, walking embodiments of madness and malice. When Raksha roam Tikor, nothing but sheer horror and terror follow in their wake.

There is often nothing subtle about their appearance or their hunting methods. Raksha come in various shapes and varieties, as each one is a unique spawn of evil reflections. One thing they do have in common is their sheer size. After consuming a host, they warp and mold the host body into hulking, leering monsters of flesh and bone. They care nothing for human life or decorum, nor do they care about nature's balance and role. They want only the warm feeling of blood splashing on their bodies. They will stalk town streets and city fairways in the hunt for flesh. Their hunger cannot be stopped, and often, neither can they.

\* \* \*

There have only been a handful of confirmed sightings of Raksha in recorded history. The validity of these sightings leaves no question as to the size and goriness of their terror sprees. They are

VOLUME 1: TIKOR, THE BEGINNING

often so public that they leave searing memories on the survivors for years to come.

The most infamous Raksha encounter was committed by a horror named Obalu the Ravenous in the town of Ghinor, Garuda. It's unknown who its host originally was, but the locals remember the blood-curdling howl that pierced the calm Garuda night upon its birth. The living nightmare went sprinting full force through the town streets, snatching up anyone unfortunate enough to cross his path.

Obalu cackled as he impaled the helpless victims upon his hellish hunting spear that he had brought with him from the dread dimension, Beneath It All. The local Celestial Shields attempted to subdue the hulking fiend but were instead turned into bloody splotches on sight.

With power and fierceness never seen before, Obalu was left unmatched. Through the night, he systematically ran from house to house with wanton slaughter. Members of the Divinity in the area quietly and mysteriously disappeared, unwilling to tangle with the Raksha. He went on to terrorize the villages of western and central Garuda for almost 50 years.

Many aspiring heroes and upstart Celestial Shields attempted to slay Obalu, but all died horribly. This slaughter continued until the Order finally launched a massive campaign against the hellspawn. A full regiment of the Divine Order of the Phoenix's finest soldiers mobilized to end Obalu's reign of terror.

\* \* \*

When the soldiers entered the fiend's lair, the monstrous creature was waiting for them on a mound of over 27000 skulls, every single one of them meticulously picked clean to the bone. The only visible marks were the scoring left by Obalu's teeth. Approximately 1500 men descended on the scene to end the demon. When the bloody battle ended, Obalu laid dead, along with nearly 1200 of the elite force.

35

BRANDON DIXON

Obalu the Ravenous is often used as a grim reminder that there are not only gods on Tikor, but demons as well. Creatures from Beneath It All have power unlike anything imagined, even in a world of magic. The time they spend in the abyss gives them un-heard-of abilities along with a seemingly endless supply of Ether. No knows exactly what the dark dimension holds, but what is clear is that more abominations like Obalu wait for the chance to feed their ravenous appetites.

*The thing that haunts me the most about that day isn't even all the death. We were all more than prepared to die that day. You had to be deaf and dumb to not hear the stories. So, yea, no one expected to come back alive. But we wanted to protect our land, and I wanted to protect my family. So like I said, it wasn't all the death that stuck with me. Though I do miss many of my brothers and sisters that died that day.*

*What haunts me really was its cackle. Every time he fell a sol-dier, he would let out this laugh that sounded like metal grinding on metal. It would rear its head back and just...laugh at us. That damn thing died with a smile on its face. As if he knew it wasn't the end.*

— PRIME SHIELD ARJANI

EXCERPT FROM "THE UNENDING HUNGER: THE 50-YEAR
SPREE OF OBALU, RAKSHA OF HUNGER"

It's hard to say whether or not Beneath It All has any sort of geography. No living soul has traveled to the realm and returned to tell the tale. Many Diviners and researchers even posit that it's impossible to go to Beneath It All. More so, even if feasible, why would anyone want to? The dark dimension does, however, affect the geography of Tikor in several ways.

## VOLUME 1: TIKOR, THE BEGINNING

During the winter, Tikor is farther from the primary sun, Ila, and closer to the second sun, Adume. Consequently, monster activity spikes as the season creeps closer toward winter. In the final few days before the winter solstice, outbreaks of Xavian's Touch peak on Tikor.

Diviners and Spirit Mediums will often cease communicating across the veil, for the dangers of unwanted passengers become too much for any but the most elite users of Ether. No one has ever bothered to wonder why these outbreaks occur, as the answer is quite plain.

The closer Tikor moves toward the cursed second sun, the thinner the protection from Xavian's plane becomes.

\* \* \*

There's a spot where the ocean currents meet in the vast waters of the Grand Divide. A whirling cyclone and temperature fluctuations make the area nearly impossible to sail through. Since the beginning of nautical travel, humans have learned to navigate around the large swath of treacherous waters.

Few adventurous and/or unlucky sailors have traveled close enough to see the inside of the spiral and survived, and they all swear upon the same thing. A strange beam of light shines at the center of the ominous 500-mile wide dark spiral. It seems to pass through the water and down into something else.

Records often noted that Raksha appear closer to the coast than inland, and whispers abound that the Dark Spiral contains more than just erratic weather—it conceals a portal to the realm of horror, Beneath It All.

# GLOSSARY OF MAJOR TERMS

**Beneath It All** – A separation pocket dimension where Xavian is sealed

**Ether** – The name for the energy that powers all life.

**Garuda** – The largest nation in the Northern Hemisphere. Home to The Divinity and controlled by The Divine Order of the Phoenix

**Etherforce** – The name for the natural occurring flow of Ether

**Ishvana** – An ancient creation god that is responsible for creating Tikor and much of its life. Sacrificed herself to seal Xavian.

**Hekan** - The name of magic in Tikor

**Raksha** – Ravenous monsters created by Xavian, sealed in Beneath It All

**The Divinity** – The general name for all the deities of Garuda. Also the specific name for a group of the oldest and most revered of Garuda's deities.

The Longest Night - The finale to a massive war between Garuda and Vinyata. Often referred to as the End of Era War.

**Vinyata** – The largest nation in the Southern Hemisphere. Home to The Four Pillars and controlled by The Republic of Vinyata.

**Xavian** – An ancient corruption god responsible for the corruption of the Elementals. Sealed away in Beneath It all.

# BOOKS IN THIS SERIES

*Chronicles of Tikor*

## The Bank Heist

Mustaf was having a normal day until the Killer Krew walked into his bank. The unofficial king of pirates, Nubia, is looking for something. And when she wants something, she gets it. Accompanied by her three Vice-Captains, the foursome are the most feared pirates on Tikor.

Will Mustaf survive this bank heist?

And what could the Killer Krew want in his bank?

## Four Stages

*Content Warning. This story deals with Alcoholism and shades of domestic abuse and implied violence*

A Spirit Medium from an elite division known as The Eyes of Garuda was commissioned to help in the investigation of a grisly quadruple homicide. The investigators assigned were baffled by the case. What they uncovered during the Mediums vision would change everything.

This vision would give the first glimpse into Xavian's Touch, a deadly mixture of curse and disease that links the victim to The

Withering King himself, Xavian.

The following is a re-telling of what the Medium saw that fateful day.

The Four Stages of Xavian's Touch

Stage 1 - Infection
Stage 2 - Host Preparation
Stage 3 - Mental Degradation
Stage 4 – The Invitation

# BOOKS BY THIS AUTHOR

## The Summit Of Kings, Battle For The Supreme Jalen: A Swordsfall Rpg Adventure

The Summit of Kings is a 2 – 4 player one-shot set in the Swordsfall universe. It can be played in several different ways. You can play it as a fun one-shot with your group, or an amusing detour for the Jalen in your Swordsfall group. Or, with a bit of homebrewing, an adventure in your system of choice. Either way, the goal is to have a unique experience of a classic rap battle of your table.

The Summit Of Kings
Once a year there is a special, one of a kind tournament held on the beautiful coast of The Isle. The Summit of Kings. A yearly battle where the top Jalens from around the world are invited to find out who is the best in straight oratorial combat. The only way to get into the Summit is through a special invite. Regardless of how well you place at The Summit, just the act of receiving an invite is considered a prestigious honor. The worldwide Jalen organization, The Sixteen, keep track of the millions of wordsages around Tikor. When the list goes out, the people listen. So, after spending months powering through the tales, speeches, and recordings of current Jalens, the Hot List is formed. The tournament set.

Over 10,000 people flock to the private beach, Boogie Cove, and the town that surrounds it, South Onyx, to witness the awesome battle. The partially secluded vista is the perfect backdrop for the lyrical battle. Owned by the reclusive Grandmaster Jalen,

Flayshe, it serves as a gorgeous backdrop for the lyrical tournament.

Who Will Be Crowned The Wordsmith?
The rules are simple. One on One, Jalen vs Jalen, Winner Takes All. Each Jalen takes there turn delivering the most crowd thrilling rap possible while the other patiently watches, careful to maintain a neutral face. They each vie for the roar of the crowd and the growing look of defeat on their foes face. Each summit battle lasts for three rounds with the winner being the best out of two.

Includes Character Sheets
Summit of Kings comes with it's own character sheets. And not just any, but the fancy kind. You can print them as normal or use your favorite PDF software to enter in the values on the sheet itself.

Printable (Black & White and Color)
Fillable (Black & White and Color)

# ABOUT THE AUTHOR

## Brandon Dixon

Brandon lives in the Portland area of Oregon with his other half, Ashley. When he's not obsessed with Swordsfall, he works fruitlessly on completing his burgeoning Steam game library.

Connect with Swordsfall:
WEBSITE: swordsfall.com
PATREON: patreon.com/swordsfall
TWITTER: twitter.com/swordsfall1
FACEBOOK: facebook.com/swordsfallrpg
INSTAGRAM: instagram.com/swordsfallrpg

Made in the USA
Middletown, DE
08 November 2020